THANKSGIVING
POEMS

THANKSGIVING POEMS

SELECTED BY

MYRA COHN LIVINGSTON

ILLUSTRATED BY

STEPHEN GAMMELL

Holiday House / New York

To the Chapros: Tamara, Fania, Nicholas, and Myron

Text copyright © by Myra Cohn Livingston
Illustrations copyright © 1985 by Stephen Gammell
All rights reserved
Printed in the United States of America
First Edition

Library of Congress Cataloging in Publication Data
Main entry under title:

Thanksgiving poems.

   Summary: A collection of poems expressing thanks-
giving from a variety of sources including American
Indian and the Bible.
   1. Thanksgiving Day—Juvenile poetry.   2. Children's
poetry. [1. Thanksgiving Day—Poetry.   2. Poetry—
Collections]   I. Livingston, Myra Cohn.   II. Gammell,
Stephen, ill.
PN6110.T6T48   1985   808.81′933   85-762
ISBN 0-8234-0570-2

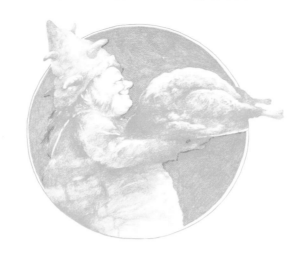

CONTENTS

AT THE FIRST THANKSGIVING
Plymouth, 1621

From friendly Squanto, wise in all things wild,
    We found out where the fattest codfish flash.
    To mingle beans and corn in succotash
We learned. We learned as though we were one child.

Today we lay our feast on maple planks
    Before Chief Massasoit and ninety braves.
    Now out of barrels bound by stout oak staves
We draw a drink to raise in heartfelt thanks

For turkeycock, ripe pumpkin, squash, and gourd,
    For stalks that stand all ears in heavy row,
    For fallow deer that round the woodlands go——
Praise to thee, Lord!

By winter winds whose edges carve like knives
    Our numbers have been pared.
    Now we who have been spared
Thank the Good Lord who took but half our lives.

X. J. KENNEDY

THE FIRST THANKSGIVING

Until the first houses could be built at Plymouth Colony, the captain of the May-flower stayed in the harbor and allowed the Pilgrims to live on board the ship.

For a long time
all we knew was the hiss
and heave of the sea
the empty shore.

Our little ship
has such a springtime name—
MAYFLOWER—like an armful
of bright blooms
from the garden!

But rocking there last fall
in the cold harbor
we wondered if a single
flower
ever grew in this hard land.

We sat chained
to the long dark days
until a warm wind
twisted sunlight through our hair
beat down on the new
rooftops.
It filled the woods with
mayflowers
and pulled green leaves
of corn
up from the earth.

Now summer has come
and gone, and we have
survived.
We give thanks.
The wind and the sea
are cold again
but fire blazes on the hearth
and the harvest is golden
in our hands.

BARBARA JUSTER ESBENSEN

10

SONG OF THE OSAGE WOMAN

Footprints I make!	Smoke arises from burning of the old stalks.
Footprints I make!	The soil lies mellowed.
Footprints I make!	The little hills stand in rows.
Footprints I make!	Lo, the little hills have turned gray.
Footprints I make!	Lo, the hills are in the light of day.
Footprints I make!	Lo, I come to the sacred act.
Footprints I make!	Give me one grain, two, three, four.
Footprints I make!	Give me five, six, the final number seven.
Footprints I make!	Lo, the tender stalk breaks the soil.
Footprints I make!	Lo, the stalk stands amidst the day.
Footprints I make!	Lo, the blades spread in the winds.
Footprints I make!	Lo, the stalks stand firm and upright.
Footprints I make!	Lo, the blades sway in the winds.
Footprints I make!	Lo, the stalk stands jointed.
Footprints I make!	Lo, the plant has blossomed.
Footprints I make!	Lo, the blades sigh in the wind.
Footprints I make!	Lo, the ears branch from the stalk.
Footprints I make!	Lo, I pluck the ears.
Footprints I make!	Lo, there is joy in my house.
Footprints I make!	Lo, the day of fulfillment.

OSAGE INDIAN

This song is sung in honor of the soil as it is prepared for the sacred act of planting corn in the seven blessed hills. It honors the stages of growth, the bearing of fruit, and the harvest that is the reward of duty and joy.

From SONGS IN THE GARDEN
OF THE HOUSE GOD

The sacred blue corn-seed I am planting,
In one night it will grow and flourish,
In one night the corn increases,
In the garden of the House God.

The sacred white corn-seed I am planting,
In one day it will grow and ripen,
In one day the corn increases,
In its beauty it increases.

NAVAHO INDIAN

COME, YE THANKFUL PEOPLE, COME

Come, ye thankful people, come,
Raise the song of harvest-home:
All is safely gathered in.
Ere the winter storms begin:
God, our Maker, doth provide
For our wants to be supplied;
Come to God's own temple, come,
Raise the song of harvest-home.

GEORGE J. ELVEY

JOY OF AN IMMIGRANT, A THANKSGIVING

Like a bird grown weak in a land
where it always rains
and where all the trees have died,
I have flown long and long
to find sunlight pouring over branches
and leaves. I have journeyed, oh God,
to find a land where I can build a dry nest,
a land where my song can echo.

EMANUEL DI PASQUALE

15

SAMANTHA SPEAKING

Dear God: My name's Samantha, and I'm seven.
In Sunday School today we talked of Heaven—
At least our Teacher did. She said nice things
About the place—Where is it? Folded wings
Are what (she told us twice) you wear up there
Where people walk on clouds; clouds float on air.
Well, now I'm in my room. I've shut the door
To say some things that I've not said before.
Thanksgiving is tomorrow. Teacher thought
That we should think about it; that we ought
To itemize (she actually said *name*)
Some things that You have given us. I came
Straight home and, after supper, got a pad
And put down this and that. If You can add,
You'll find they come to what I hoped—to seven,
Which is my age; which also rhymes with Heaven.
Health, sight, hearing, speech, mind, for a starter.
That leaves me two to go. If I were smarter,
I'd know *which* two; one could be just the Earth,
For that is what You gave me at my birth.
Still, I don't own it, though it's part of me.
Friendship is better, for in friends we see
So much: taste, courage, kindness, trust. The key
To friendship, though, I guess is love; so I
Choose love. And You won't mind if I add sky?
Heaven's up there; we *do* say *God on High*.
So there's my seven that I'm thankful for.
Dear God, I *mean* it! Thank You, God, once more.

DAVID McCORD

17

THE TURKEY'S WATTLE

Said the Turtle to the Turkey
Every time he came to visit,
"There's a funny hunk of wrinkle
Where your chin should be, what is it?"

Said the Turkey to the Turtle,
"Oh, this rubber decoration?
Heavens, no, I wouldn't tell you
'Cause it makes for conversation.

At Thanksgiving during dinner—
It's my relative they're carving!—
Silly People sit around and
Stuff them*selves* as if they're starving,

And you know the only question
They can think of while they visit?
'Say, that funny hunk of wrinkle
Round a Turkey's chin, what is it?!' "

J. PATRICK LEWIS

18

GOBBLEDY-GOBBLE

How they laughed!

    "He's so scrawny.
    Scrawny! Scrawny!" they taunt me.
    "Not handsome and brawny.
    He's ugly as sin."
So gobbledy-gob-
ble, I'm not with the mob
because of the shape that I'm in.
    "The worst on the block.
    A disgrace to the flock."
They're ashamed to admit
they're my kin.

Well, sometimes they hurt
('Twould be nice to be purt-
y.), but common sense says
"You're a winner."
For on Thanksgiving Day
they have all gone away
to be somebody's good-looking dinner.

                         FELICE HOLMAN

MAKE A JOYFUL NOISE UNTO THE LORD

Make a joyful noise unto the Lord, all ye lands,
Serve the Lord with gladness:
Come before his presence with singing.
Know ye that the Lord he is God:
It is he that hath made us, and not we ourselves;
We are his people, and the sheep of his pasture.
Enter into his gates with thanksgiving,
And into his courts with praise:
Be thankful unto him, and bless his name.
For the Lord is good; his mercy is everlasting;
And his truth endureth to all generations.

PSALM 100
THE HOLY BIBLE
King James Version

FAMILY REUNION

Thanksgiving Day! Our family
Arrives from far and near—
"Why, Leland! My, how tall you've grown!"
Cries Aunt, year after year.

She always stands me back to back
Up next to Cousin Rhoda.
The tall folks sip pink sparkly wine;
Us kids, raspberry soda.

Creak! go nutcrackers, building mounds
Of wrinkled shells from walnuts.
When Uncle Dom plays dominos
He cheats (and drives us *all* nuts).

Down come rosemary, sage, and thyme
From spicy-smelling shelves——
We stuff a bird with all that stuff
And soon we stuff ourselves.

X. J. KENNEDY

PASS THE PLATE

Pass the plate,
another serving.
Who else here
is *more* deserving?

> Did my chores,
> (Some white meat, please).
> Homework's neat,
> (With fresh green peas).
> Dog's been fed,
> (Some candied yam).
> Plants all watered,
> (Slice of ham).
> Bed is made,
> (A piece of pie).
> Who deserves as much
>   as I?

Pass the plate,
another serving.
Who else here
is more deserving?

JANE YOLEN

JAKE O'LEARY'S THANKSGIVING

When Jake O'Leary
Thanksgiving Day
Was having lunch
With his Auntie Mae
And later on
When dessert came by
Was given his private
Pumpkin pie

And hated the filling,
Hated the crust
And couldn't eat it
And knew he must . . .
In order to get it
Out of sight,
He gobbled the pie
In ONE BIG BITE.

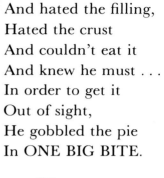

Though gulping the pie
Was far from easy
And Jake O'Leary
Felt stuffed and queasy,
He forced himself
(As a person does)
To thank his auntie
Whose pie it was,

But found his thanks
Were a sad mistake
When Mae, his auntie,
Remarked to Jake:
"It's easy to see
With half an eye
You're crazy about
My pumpkin pie."

And off she hurried
On flying feet
And brought him another
Pie to eat.

KAYE STARBIRD

27

SICILIAN THANKSGIVING ON THE FEAST OF SAINT JOHN THE BAPTIST
(Marking the End of Summer)

I pull a baby crab
off a seaweed-rich rock
and let it run on my hands,
and I see God. I see God
in millions of lights
dancing in the sea and air.
Hear Him in the wail of street vendor
selling parsley and basil.
Hear Him in my own squeals
as I'm outrun by a foaming wave.
Feel Him in the smooth circling
of swallows,
in the quick beat of pigeons
landing in the cracks of clay roofs.
And I see God in the jasmine flower:
white and spread out as a gown
that dawn winds lift.

EMANUEL DI PASQUALE

CAT: THANKSGIVING

Now, in lean November,
The silent houses
Huddle in despair,
Every front porch
Forlorn, abandoned to
Its mailbox and its mat—
A patch of cold brown
Stubble, uncomfortable
Even to the cat;

But we, indoors,
Have company and clamor,
Fruitfulness and fire,
Luxury to spare—
So that when she
Runs in, complaining,
We offer her our laps,
And stroke her chilly fur,
And feed her turkey-scraps.

VALERIE WORTH

GIVING THANKS   GIVING THANKS

Giving thanks   giving thanks
for rain and rainbows
sun and sunsets
cats and catbirds
larks and larkspur

giving thanks   giving thanks
for cows and cowslips
eggs and eggplants
stars and starlings
dogs and dogwood

giving thanks   giving thanks
for watercress on river banks
for necks and elbows knees and shanks
for towers basins pools and tanks
for pumps and handles lifts and cranks

giving thanks   giving thanks
for ropes and coils and braids and hanks
for jobs and jokes and plots and pranks
for whistles bells and plinks and clanks
giving giving giving THANKS

EVE MERRIAM

31

ACKNOWLEDGMENTS

Grateful acknowledgment is made to the following poets, whose work was especially commissioned for this book:

Emanuel di Pasquale for "Joy of an Immigrant, a Thanksgiving" and "Sicilian Thanksgiving on the Feast of Saint John the Baptist." Copyright © 1985 by Emanuel di Pasquale.

Barbara Juster Esbensen for "The First Thanksgiving." Copyright © 1985 by Barbara Juster Esbensen.

Felice Holman for "Gobbledy-Gobble." Copyright © 1985 by Felice Holman.

X. J. Kennedy for "At the First Thanksgiving" and "Family Reunion." Copyright © 1985 by X. J. Kennedy.

J. Patrick Lewis for "The Turkey's Wattle." Copyright © 1985 by J. Patrick Lewis.

David McCord for "Samantha Speaking." Copyright © 1985 by David McCord.

Eve Merriam for "Giving Thanks   Giving Thanks." Copyright © 1985 by Eve Merriam. Reprinted by permission of Patricia Ayers. All rights reserved.

Kaye Starbird for "Jake O'Leary's Thanksgiving." Copyright © 1985 by Kaye Starbird. Reprinted by permission of Ray Lincoln Literary Agency.

Valerie Worth for "Cat: Thanksgiving." Copyright © 1985 by Valerie Worth Bahlke.

Jane Yolen for "Pass the Plate." Copyright © 1985 by Jane Yolen. Reprinted by permission of Curtis Brown, Ltd.

Grateful acknowledgment is also made for the following reprints:

Farrar, Straus & Giroux, Inc. for excerpt from "Songs in the Garden of the House God" from *In the Trail of the Wind*, edited by John Bierhorst. Copyright © 1971 by John Bierhorst. Reprinted by permission of Farrar, Straus & Giroux, Inc.

Smithsonian Institution Press for "Song of the Osage Woman" adapted by Myra Cohn Livingston from Forty-fifth annual report of the Bureau of American Ethnology to the Secretary of the Smithsonian Institution, 1927–28, "The Osage Tribe: Rite of the Wa-xó-be," by Francis La Flesche. Smithsonian Institution, Washington, D.C. 1930. Adaptation copyright © 1985 by Myra Cohn Livingston.